This Book Belongs To:

To my *wildlings*.
Home is where your
LEGO Bricks drop.
And to you, my friends.

The Big Adventures Of A Little Tree
Tree Finds Friendship

Library of Congress Control Number: 2020921143

First Edition 2020
www.thepassionatepeanut.com
Member of the Alliance of Independent Authors

Publisher's Cataloging-in-Publication data

Names: Springer, Nadja, author. I Rand-Bell, Tilia, illustrator.
Title: The big adventures of a little tree
[by Nadja Springer; illustrated by Tilia Rand-Bell].
Description: New Jersey: Nadja Springer, 2020
Summary: Tree has all that he needs, a beautiful home and a loving family.
Still, Tree yearns to wander – and to explore the world.
Identifiers: LCCN: 2020921143
ISBN: 978-1-7360281-2-4 (Hardcover)
978-1-7360281-0-0 (pbk.)
978-1-7360281-1-7 (ebook)
Subjects: LCSH Trees--Juvenile fiction. I Friendship--Juvenile fiction.
Stories in rhyme. I CYAC Trees--Fiction. I Friendship--Fiction.
BISAC JUVENILE FICTION / General
Classification: LCC PZ7.1 .S67 Big 2020 I DDC [E]--dc23

THE BIG ADVENTURES OF A Little TREE

TREE FINDS Friendship

written by
Nadja Springer

Illustrated by
Tilia Rand-Bell

Down by the shore,
where the sea turtles are,
there lives a *small tree*,
the greenest by far.

He's spent his whole life
with his sisters and brothers,
but yearns to go *wander*
and meet many others.

He tries hard to leave,
but his roots are so deep.

He can't even walk,
and he surely can't leap.

Tree comes up with a **plan** and calls out to the wind,

"I'm about to go places that I've never been!"

By pulling his
branches,
birds help him
to walk.

"It works! Tree is moving!"
they *excitedly*
squawk.

The animals
watch as Tree waves
to the crowd.
"I'm seeking *adventure*,"
he cries, feeling proud.

Tree reaches a meadow,
      sees **children** at play.

He asks to join in,
      but they all run away.

That is,
all except one,

who steps forward to talk.

"How did you get here?
I know trees *can't walk*."

Tree tells her that *birds*
simply tugged and then lifted,

'til his roots and his branches

all finally shifted.

The girl is *surprised*,

yelling, "Guys, come and see!"

"It's hard to believe,
my new friend is a *tree*!"

The children all giggle.
The birds flutter by.

He's made lots of *friends*
in the blink of an eye.

Now Tree and the *children*,
love playing
all day,

running free in the *meadow* 'til Tree heard one child say...

"Oh! *Winter* is coming!
We must say goodbye."

How will Tree get home?
There's a **tear** in his eye.

"I'm sorry, my friends,
there's no time left to roam.
With winter arriving,

I need help getting *home!*"

The children love Tree.
They all give him a hug.
"We will take you back there.
We can *pull*. We can *tug*."

They gather their bikes,

and they pull Tree along.

Their *love* and their *friendship*

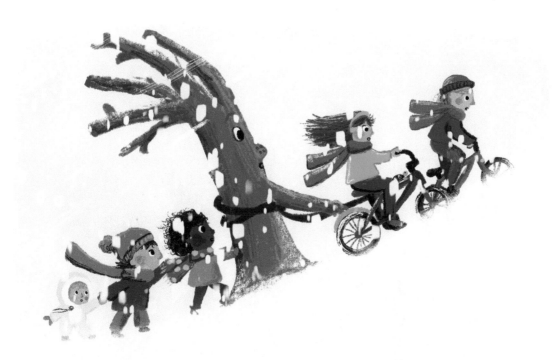

are making them *strong*.

Tree's brothers and sisters
are happy to see...
all the **children**, and learn
how they took care of Tree.

As Tree hugs goodbye,
there's no need to feel grim.
"When summer returns,
please come back for a *swim*!"

"I will always remember
the friends I hold *dear.*

They will stay in my *heart*
year after year!"

Down by the shore,
where the sea turtles are,
there lives a tree with a *smile*
you can see from afar.

Did you enjoy Tree's adventure?

It would be **"tree-riffic"** if you can leave your review on Amazon or Goodreads. Your feedback is so important and is very much *appreciated*.

Hop over to
www.ThePassionatePeanut.com
for some fun games with Tree and his friends. Grab your *free* downloads and more!

THE PASSIONATE PEANUT

✱ SPRING JOKE
What season is it when you are on a trampoline?

Spring-time!

✱ Have a picnic

✱ Go on a family hike

✱ Plant seeds

✱ Notice the trees budding

Things to do in the SPRING

Things to do in the SUMMER

 Walk bare foot

 Go swimming

Create sidewalk chalk art

 Blow bubbles

SUMMER JOKE
What does the sun drink out of?

Sunglasses.

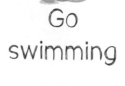 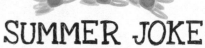 

Things to do in the
FALL

Dive into a pile of leaves

Make a forest crown using leaves

Fly a kite

Jump in puddles

FALL JOKE
Why do birds fly south in the fall?

Because it's too far to walk!

WINTER JOKE
What's a snowman's favorite drink?

Ice tea.

Build a snowman

Create a bird feeder from pine cones

Make a campfire and have s'mores

Throw snowballs

Things to do in the
WINTER

The Author

Nadja Springer is a translator, a member of the Alliance of Independent Authors and a haunter of bookstores. She's the wife of her own personal rock star and the mother of three curious free-range girls and one hairy teenage Golden Retriever. She has lived in the middle of nowhere, in the center of everything, and currently on the East Coast of the United States.

You can also chat with Nadja on Instagram: @thepassionatepeanut

The *Illustrator*

Tilia Rand-Bell is an Illustrator from Bristol, working on many wonderful books all over the world. When she's not drawing, she spends her time day dreaming about new places to travel, or finding new places to eat. She also keeps everything at arms reach in case her cat falls asleep on her.

You can learn more about Tilia by visiting her corner of the internet, www.Cosmo-Creative.com, or on Instagram: @cosmocreativedesign

CPSIA information can be obtained
at www.ICGtesting.com
Printed in the USA
BVHW020222100221
599791BV00007B/15